Jellybean Book

# The Berenstain Bears
# GET THE
# SCREAMIES

## Stan & Jan Berenstain

### Random House 🏠 New York

ISBN: 0-679-89235-4 (trade) ; 0-679-99235-9 (lib. bdg.) Library of Congress Catalog Card Number: 98-65547
www.randomhouse.com/kids/    www.berenstainbears.com
Printed in the United States of America  10 9 8 7 6 5 4 3 2 1
JELLYBEAN BOOKS is a trademark of Random House, Inc.

"I'm going to the mall," said Mama Bear as she put on her dress-up hat. "And you may come, provided..."

"Provided what?" asked cubs Brother and Sister.

"*Provided,*" said Mama, "that you behave properly and remain calm throughout the trip—especially if we should happen to go past the toy store."

"Yes, Mama," said Brother. "We shall behave properly and remain calm throughout the trip."

"Even," said Sister, "if we should happen to go past the toy store."

Mama's first mall stop was Buttons and Bows, a store that sold buttons, bows, thread, yarn, and everything else that had to do with sewing and mending.

Mama checked her list and bought some spools of thread. Brother and Sister behaved properly and remained calm, as they had promised. Buttons and Bows was nowhere near the toy store.

Mama's next stop was the hardware store. Mama checked her list and bought a package of hacksaw blades and some drill bits for Papa.

Brother and Sister behaved properly and remained calm. The toy store was nowhere in sight.

The next stop was Bed and Bath. Mama checked her list and bought a back brush and some pillowcases. Brother and Sister looked all around. Where *was* that toy store?

That's when Mama took a wrong turn.
To the delight of the cubs and to the dismay
of Mama, there it was: the toy store!

"The toy store! The toy store!"
cried the cubs, jumping up and down.

"I want a new Bearbie!" cried Sister.
"I want a new video game!" cried Brother.
"Hmm," said Mama, looking at her list.
"I don't see anything here about toys."

Now the cubs were jumping up and
down and screaming.

It was the worst case of the screaming screamies Mama had ever seen. The other Bears at the mall were impressed, too.

Mama had had enough. She began to jump up and down and scream. She even fell to the ground kicking and screaming. It was the worst case of the screaming screamies the cubs had ever seen. They watched for a while.

"Can we leave now?" asked Brother.

"Why, of course," said Mama, picking herself up and dusting herself off. And they left.